JAMES THURBER

THE TIGER
WHO WOULD BE KING

ILLUSTRATED BY
JOOHEE YOON

ENCHANTED LION BOOKS
NEW YORK

One morning the tiger woke up in the jungle and told his mate that

he was king of beasts.

"Leo, the lion, is king of beasts," she said.

"We need a change," said the tiger.
"The creatures are crying for a change."

The tigress listened but she could hear
no crying, except that of her cubs.

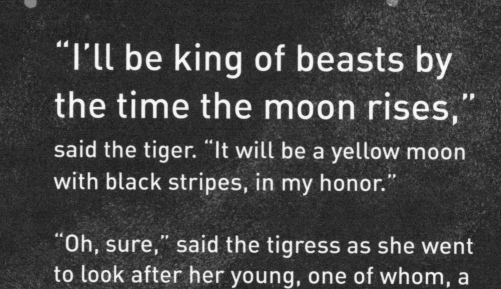

"I'll be king of beasts by the time the moon rises," said the tiger. "It will be a yellow moon with black stripes, in my honor."

"Oh, sure," said the tigress as she went to look after her young, one of whom, a male, very like his father, had got an imaginary thorn in his paw.

The tiger prowled through the jungle
till he came to the lion's den.

"Come out," he roared, "and
greet the king of beasts!
The king is dead,
long live the king!"

Inside the den, the lioness woke her mate.
"The king is here to see you," she said.

"What king?" he inquired, sleepily.
"The king of beasts," she said.

"I am the king of beasts,"

roared Leo, and he charged out of the den to defend his crown against the pretender.

It was a terrible fight, and it lasted until the setting of the sun.

All the animals of the jungle joined in,

some taking the side of the tiger

and others the side of the lion.

Every creature from the aardvark
to the zebra took part in the struggle to
overthrow the lion or to repulse the tiger,

and some did not know
which they were fighting for,

and some fought for both,

and some fought whoever
was nearest, and some fought
for the sake of fighting.

"What are we fighting for?" someone asked the aardvark.

"The old order," said the aardvark.

"What are we dying for?"
someone asked the zebra.
"The new order,"
said the zebra.

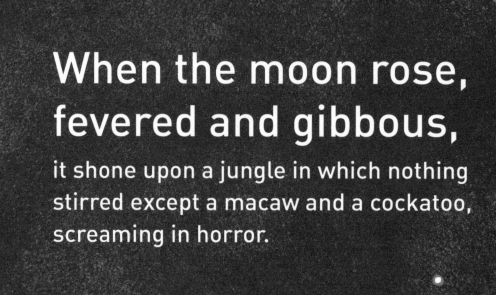

When the moon rose, fevered and gibbous,

it shone upon a jungle in which nothing stirred except a macaw and a cockatoo, screaming in horror.

All the beasts were dead except the tiger, and his days were numbered and his time was ticking away. He was monarch of all he surveyed, but it didn't seem to mean anything.

MORAL:
You can't very well be king of beasts if there aren't any.

First Edition published 2015 by Enchanted Lion Books
351 Van Brunt Street, Brooklyn, NY 11231
All rights reserved under International and
Pan-American Copyright Conventions
A CIP record is on file with the Library of Congress
ISBN 978-1-59270-182-7
Book design: JooHee Yoon
Printed in China by South China Printing Co. Ltd.
First Printing

WWW.ENCHANTEDLIONBOOKS.COM

The artwork was created by hand drawing and the computer.
Two Pantone colors were used in the printing of this book.

Thurber House (www.ThurberHouse.org), continues the legacy of
James Thurber and has awarded the Thurber Prize for outstanding
American humor to such writers as Ian Frazier, Jon Stewart,
Alan Zweibel, Joe Keenan and Calvin Trillin.

For mom & dad